KT-151-563

Happy Christmas, Friendly Dragon

Ron Maris

Hurry up! Santa's waiting for you.

WALKER BOOKS
LONDON

CUMBRIA COUNTY LIBRARY

3 8003 01633 9962

For all our Jolly neighbours!

First published 1990 by Julia MacRae Books
This edition published 1992 by Walker Books Ltd
87 Vauxhall Walk, London SE11 5HJ

© 1990 Ron Maris

Printed and bound in Hong Kong by Imago

British Library Cataloguing in Publication Data
A catalogue record for this book is
available from the British Library.
ISBN 0-7445-2362-1

Santa Claus lives with Mrs Claus
in a big stone house high up
in the snowy mountains.

It is Christmas Eve and time to pack
up the presents for children everywhere.
Rebecca and Bruno have come to help.

Amelia

Delia
Linda
Susie
Carla
Emma

Julia

Sebastian

Matthew

Richard

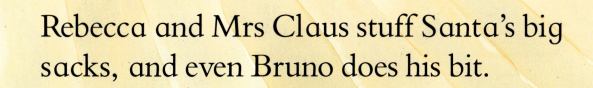

Rebecca and Mrs Claus stuff Santa's big
sacks, and even Bruno does his bit.

As far as the eye can see,
there is snow piled high.

At last Santa is able to make
his way through the snow to
the reindeer stables.

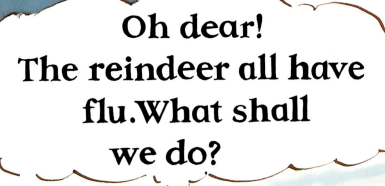

But there is a sad surprise inside.

I don't know, Mr Claus. We haven't much time.
Delia
Linda
Susie
Carla
Emma

Who will
pull the sleigh,
Mrs Claus?

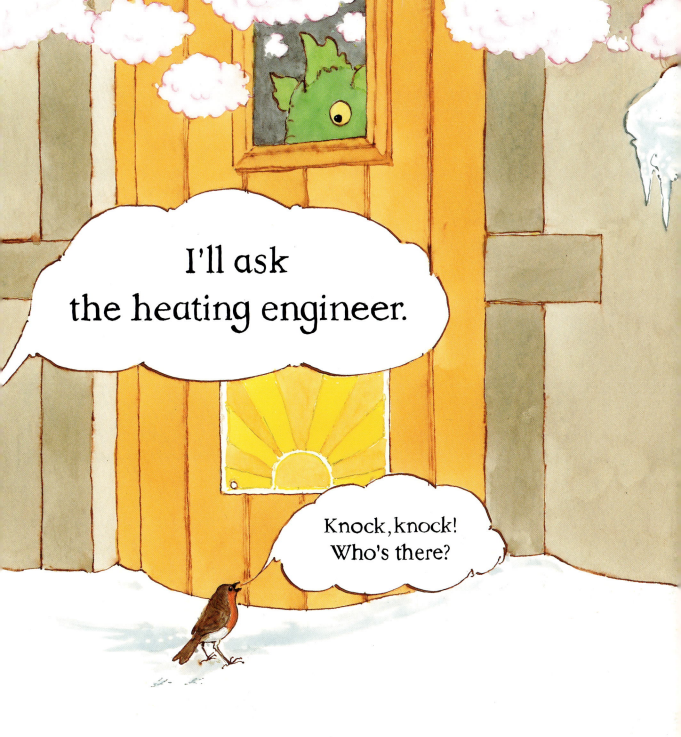

Rebecca knows exactly what to do.

Can you help us,
Friendly Dragon?

Come on,
Friendly. Lend a
claw.

Everyone gets to work.

Go, Dragon, go!
You've got a night's work to do!

Fly safely, Friendly Dragon.

Here we are,
and down we go.

Santa Claus climbs into
the very last chimney.

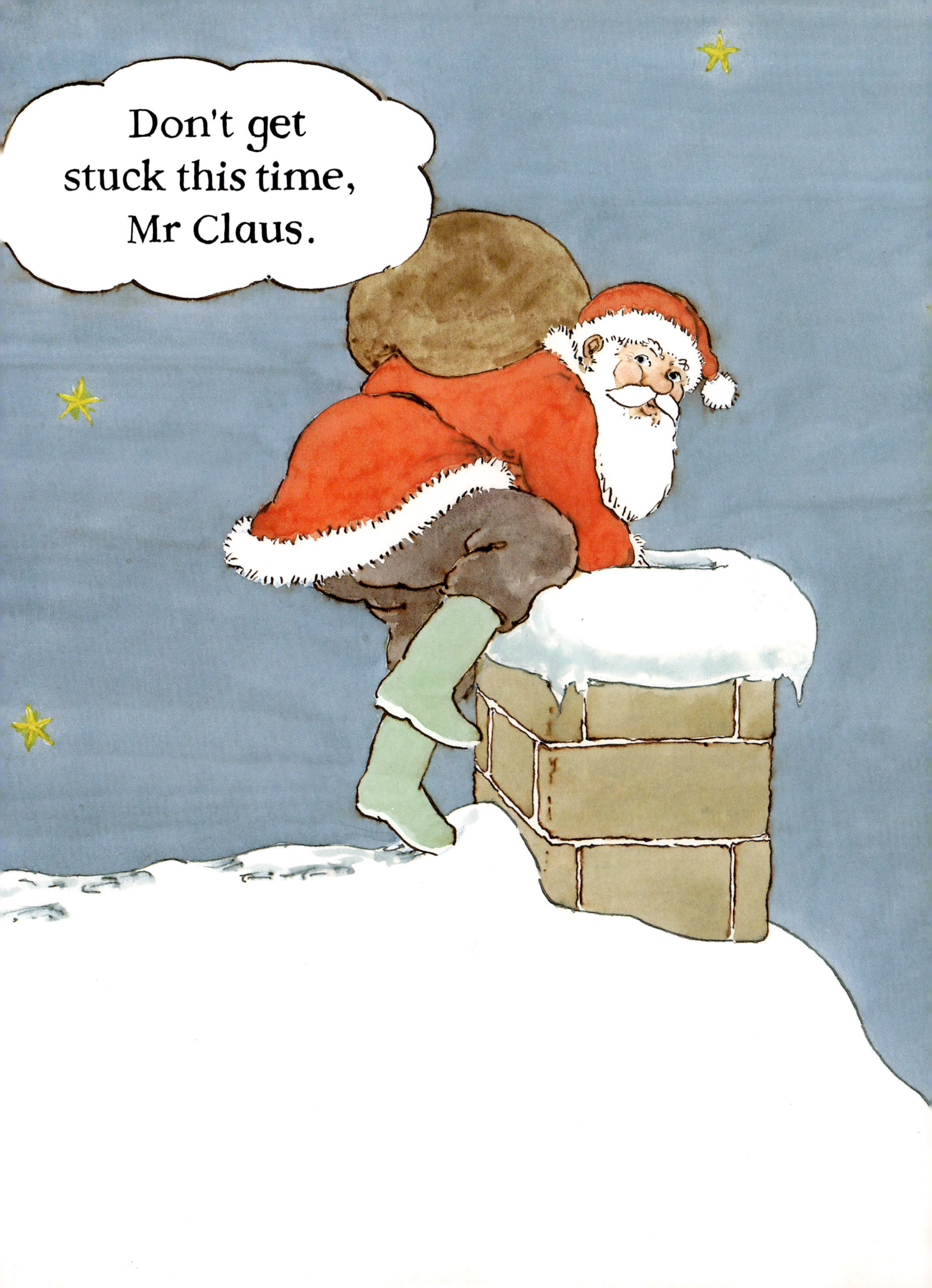
Don't get stuck this time, Mr Claus.

Friendly Dragon brings them home.

Hello,Rebecca.
We're home agai
Friendly
A dog's life isn't so bad.

Happy Christmas, Friendly Dragon!